Irish Setter
Blue Great Dane
Brittany Spaniel
German Shepherd
Yellow Labrador Retriever
Pit Bull

by

Kevin O'Malley

Crown Books for Young Readers New York

FOR DARA, WHO HAS THE PERFECT DOG

Published in the United States by Crown Books for Young Readers,
an imprint of Random House Children's Books,
a division of Penguin Random House LLC, New York.
Crown and the colophon are registered trademarks of Penguin Random House LLC.

Visit us on the Web! randomhousekids.com
Educators and librarians, for a variety of teaching tools,
visit us at RHTeachersLibrarians.com

Library of Congress Cataloging-in-Publication Data
Names: O'Malley, Kevin, 1961- author, illustrator.
Title: The perfect dog / Kevin O'Malley.
Description: First edition. | New York : Crown Books for Young Readers, [2016] | Summary:
"A girl tries to pick the perfect dog for her, but in the end, the right dog picks her"– Provided by publisher.
Identifiers: LCCN 2015029102 | ISBN 978-1-101-93441-8 (hardback) | ISBN 978-1-101-93442-5 (glb) |
ISBN 978-1-101-93443-2 (epub)
Subjects: | CYAC: Dogs–Fiction. | BISAC: JUVENILE FICTION / Animals / Dogs. |
JUVENILE FICTION / Animals / Pets. | JUVENILE FICTION / Concepts / Words.
Classification: LCC PZ7.O526 Pe 2016 | DDC [E]–dc23

The illustrations in this book were created with ink on Graphics 360 paper
with a Hunt nib and colored in Photoshop.

MANUFACTURED IN CHINA 10 9 8 7 6 5 4 3 2 1 First Edition
Random House Children's Books supports the
First Amendment and celebrates the right to read.

My parents said
we could get a dog.

The perfect dog should be **big** . . .

bigger...

biggest!

Maybe not this
big.

The perfect dog should be small . . .

smallest!
Maybe not this small.

The perfect dog
should have
LONG
hair . . .

LONGER...

LONGEST!
Maybe not this LONG.

The perfect dog should **NOT** be too . . .

Or too . . .

The perfect dog should be *fancy* . . .

fanciest!
Maybe not this fancy.

The perfect dog should be *fast*. . .

faster...

fastest!

Maybe not this *fast*.

The perfect dog should be snuggly . . .

snuggliest!
Maybe not this snuggly.

The perfect dog should **NOT** be too . . .

Or too . . .

So we went to get the perfect dog.

We finally decided the perfect dog should be . . .

HAPPY. . .

HAPPIER . . .

HAPPIEST!

But then . . .

Arf,
arf,
arf!

The perfect dog found me!

Doberman Pinscher
Bullmastiff
Corgi
Dachshund
Schnauzer
Poodle